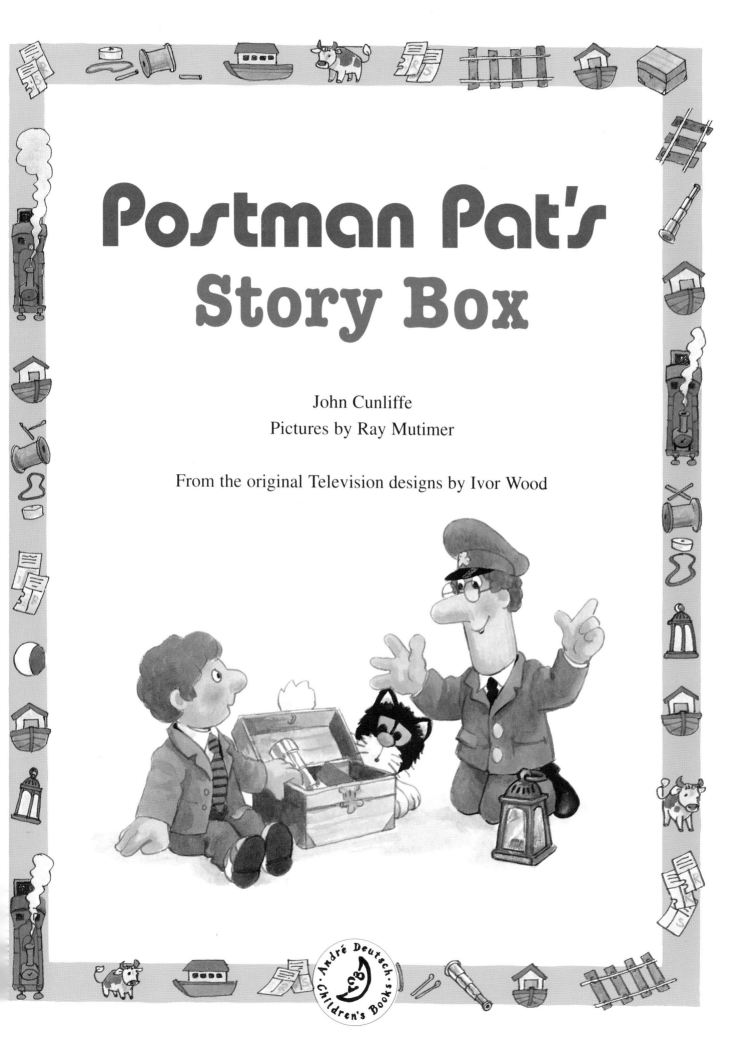

Postman Pat's Story Box

John Cunliffe

Pictures by Ray Mutimer

From the original Television designs by Ivor Wood

André Deutsch Children's Books

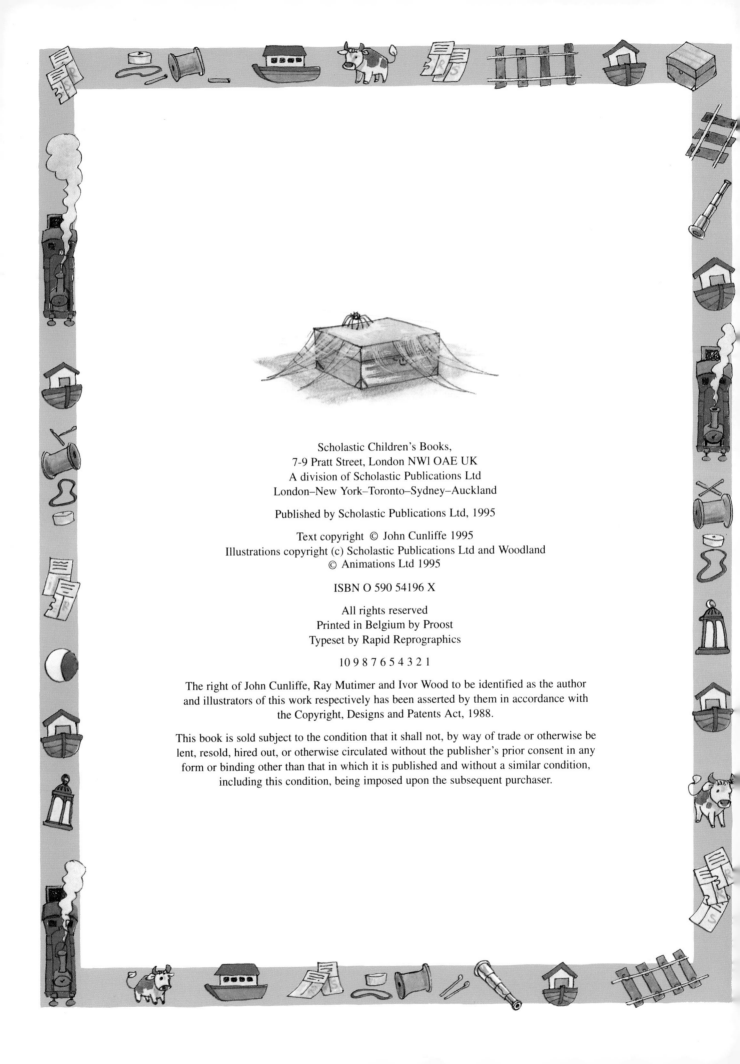

Scholastic Children's Books,
7-9 Pratt Street, London NWl OAE UK
A division of Scholastic Publications Ltd
London–New York–Toronto–Sydney–Auckland

Published by Scholastic Publications Ltd, 1995

ISBN O 590 54196 X

Contents

1. Treasure in the Attic   4

2. The Telescope   9

3. A Telescope Rescue   13

4. The Lantern Ghost Story   18

5. A Moonlight Post   23

6. A Bag of Bobbins   28

7. A Small Contraption   31

8. Tractors Galore!   34

9. A Cold Christmas   37

10. The Great Greendale Bobbin Race   43

11. The Greendale Light Railway   48

12. Along the Tracks   52

13. A Ride on a Train   55

14. The Newest Story   58

All the Stories   63

1 Treasure in the Attic

It was a wet and windy Saturday afternoon in Greendale.
It was too wet to do the gardening.
It was too wet to put the washing out.
It was too wet to go out at all.
    "What shall we do?" said Julian.
    "Read a book," said Pat.

So Julian read a book.
Pat read the Pencaster Gazette.
Sara mended the old rocking-chair.

Julian finished his book. It was still raining; coming down in spouts.
    "What can we do now?" said Julian.
    "Train-set?" said Pat.
    "I had it out on Friday," said Julian.
    "Do a jig-saw?" said Sara.
    "They all have bits missing," said Julian.
    "We could have a game of ludo," said Pat, hopefully.
    "It's boring," said Julian.
    "I know what!" said Pat.
    "What?"
    "We'll go up to the loft . . . "

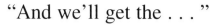

"Yes?"

"And we'll get the . . . "

"What . . . what . . . Dad?"

"We'll get the old story box out," said Pat, smiling.

"The what?"

"The old story box. When I was a lad, my grandad had one, and his dad before him. But I've no idea what might be in it. It's donkey's years since I looked in it. I'd forgotten all about it. It might be full of spiders and cobwebs and mice."

"We'd better take Jess up to the loft," said Julian. "Just in case."

"You'll never keep him out," said Pat. "I think he's tired of the rain, as well."

Pat went to get his ladder, and they climbed up into the dark and dusty loft. Jess went first, then came Pat, with his big torch, then Julian, then Sara, making sure that no-one slipped on the ladder.

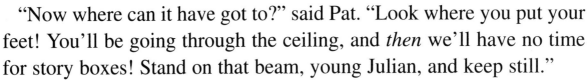

"Now where can it have got to?" said Pat. "Look where you put your feet! You'll be going through the ceiling, and *then* we'll have no time for story boxes! Stand on that beam, young Julian, and keep still."

Pat flashed his torch about in the darkness. There was a foggy dustiness that made them all sneeze. Shapes loomed up in the dim light.

"There's that old sewing-machine," said Sara. "It was supposed to be mended three Christmases back. Now *that's* something to keep Dad busy for a few wet days."

"I'll do it tomorrow. Promise," said Pat. "But, just for now, we're looking for . . . "

"There it is!" said Sara.

Pat stepped carefully across the loft to the box that Sara had spotted. It was covered in an old blanket. Pat lifted the blanket. A mouse ran out, and Jess ran after it. He lost it somewhere behind the water-tanks. When he came round the other side, he looked so funny. He had run into an old spider's web, and he was covered in rags and tags of dusty gossamer. He shook his head and sneezed, then ran back down the ladder to have a good wash.

"This isn't it," said Pat, peering into the darkness. "It's an old pram."

"Whose pram is it?" said Julian.

"It was yours," said Sara, "when you were a baby."

"A long time ago," said Pat.

"Give me a hand with this sewing-machine," said Sara.

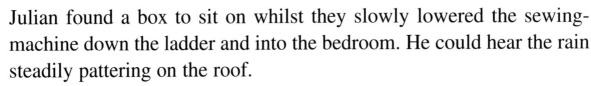

Julian found a box to sit on whilst they slowly lowered the sewing-machine down the ladder and into the bedroom. He could hear the rain steadily pattering on the roof.

"What about the story box?" he shouted down to them.

"Coming!" called Pat. He came puffing back up the ladder. "Now, then, young Julian, what's that you're sitting on? It might be the story box!"

Julian opened the lid, raising clouds of dust.

"It's only a box of old pans," he said.

"We'll have that out," said Sara.

"There's something else behind it," said Julian. "Another old box."

"You've got it!" said Pat.

"What?" said Julian. "Is it the story box?"

"It certainly is," said Pat. "I don't know how it came to be just there. Never mind. We'd best get it down this ladder. Steady as you go. Just push it towards me. Careful! Slowly does it."

Bit by bit, they moved it across the loft to the top of the ladder. Then, Pat eased it on to his shoulder, and carried it safely down to the landing. Sara was waiting with the vacuum cleaner at the ready.

"Let me do it," shouted Julian.

He vacuumed it all over, sucking up every last particle of dust.

"That's better," said Sara. "It's fit to take downstairs, now."

When the box was safely on the rug by the fire, Julian tugged at the lid.

"It won't open," he said.

"It's locked," said Pat. "Hang on, I'll soon find the key. I know I've got it somewhere. . ."

Now Pat began a longer search; opening cupboards and drawers, looking in old jars and tins, sorting out piles of buttons and rusty screws.

"Where does all this stuff come from?" said Sara. "I don't know, we'll have to have a good clear-out one of these wet days."

"Got it!" cried Pat.

"The key?" said Julian.

"For the sewing-machine," said Pat.

"Oh," said Julian.

"Here it is," said Pat. "Cheer up."

"The key?" "Yes. The story box key," said Pat, fitting a rusty old key into the lock. The lid opened with a loud groan.

"Ooooooh!" said Julian.

"Well, I don't know!" said Pat. "Fancy all this stuff being hidden away all these years."

"*I* know," said Sara. "You can get some newspaper down before you get anything out."

It was a box of treasures such as Julian had never seen before. They spread them out on the newspaper-covered carpet. Julian knew what some of the things were; a telescope, and a lantern. But there were many things that were no less than a mystery to him. Things with strange levers and buttons, and lenses to look through.

"One thing at a time," said Pat. "There's enough here to keep us busy for many and many a day. Besides, there's a story to be told about each and every article in this box."

"Where shall we begin?" said Julian.

2 The Telescope

"I'll tell you what," said Pat. "Let's just choose one thing, and put the others away for another day."

"That's a good idea," said Julian.

"You choose," said Pat.

"This," said Julian.

"The telescope," said Pat.

"Has it got a story?" said Julian.

"It certainly has," said Pat. "Not just one story; dozens. Now, if you could see just half of the things this old telescope has seen. . ."

"Tell me," said Julian.

"Well," said Pat, "this old telescope was my grandad's once. A long time ago, he lived by the sea. He was a lifeboat man."

"What did he do with his telescope?"

"He kept a lookout for boats on days just like today. When the high winds blow and the rain comes pouring down, it's really dangerous at sea. The water blows up into huge waves that can sink a fishing-boat. When Grandad saw a boat in trouble, through his telescope, he would send a rocket up into the sky. That was a signal to the men of the village to run and launch the lifeboat. Then they sailed out to rescue the fishermen from the storm. There was one time I remember him telling me about, when the telescope helped to save a dog."

"Was it in a boat?" said Julian.

"No, but it was somewhere it should never have gone," said Pat. "Grandad could hear this sound of whining and whimpering, as he walked along the beach. It was lucky that it was a calm day; he would never have heard it if the wind had been blowing. It seemed to come nearer and nearer, but he still couldn't see it. He looked out to sea, and scanned the waves with the telescope, hoping to see a little head, bobbing amongst the waves, but there was nothing more than a few gulls. Then he turned the telescope towards the cliffs, and searched up and down. There are lots of nooks and ledges on those cliffs, where the birds nest in their thousands."

"Was it there?"

"Yes, it was stuck high up on a tiny ledge of rock, and it couldn't get down."

"Like our Jess, when he got stuck up the tree," said Julian.

"Well, yes, but a good deal worse," said Pat. "The cliffs are much higher than any tree. The poor little creature must have climbed up, following some scent, and then got to a place where he couldn't turn round without falling off. He was frozen with fear, and couldn't move at all. He was almost the same colour as the cliff, so Grandad would never have spotted him without the telescope."

"Did he get him down?"

"Not Grandad himself. He was no climber; but there were some young men with climbing-gear, further along the cliff-top, and they easily got down to the dog, and brought him up. He was soon running about as though nothing had happened."

"That was good. What else did he see?"

"Oh, he often saw seals swimming in the sea, or lying out on the sand-banks. He saw a whale once. Dolphins, jumping out of the water. And, just once, a shark!"

"Ooooh!"

Pat told Julian stories about all the things that his grandad had seen through his telescope. Then they pointed the telescope out of the

10

window. He showed Julian how to look with one eye into the little round glass, down the long brass tube, and out into the rainy world.

"What can you see?" said Pat.

"Sharks," said Julian, "elephants, snakes, and a walrus."
Then it was Pat's turn.

"What can you see?" said Julian. "A fierce monster," said Pat. "I think it must be Jess, looking for a mouse."
Sara came to see.

"What can you see?" said Julian.

"The clock on the church-tower," said Sara, "and it says it's tea-time."

"Anything to be rescued?" said Julian.

"Yes," said Sara. "Hot scones, waiting to be rescued from the oven."

"Lovely," said Pat. "We'll send a rocket up."

"No need for that," said Sara. "Just get that cloth on the table."

After tea, it was dark outside, and there was nothing to be seen through the telescope. Pat polished and cleaned Grandad's old telescope, and put it by Julian's bed, so that he could see it when he went to sleep.

"Tomorrow," said Pat, "when the rain stops, we'll take the telescope up the hill, and see if we can see Ted Glen sawing his logs. But we'll have to remember the telescope rule."

"What's that?"

"Never, ever, point it at the sun."

"Why?"

"Because the sun's so hot it will hurt your eyes if you look at it through a telescope. It could even blind you," said Pat.

"I'll not forget," said Julian. "Promise. We'd better take a rocket; we might see someone to rescue."

"You never know," said Pat.

3 A Telescope Rescue

When morning came, Julian woke from a night of telescope-dreams, to see the sun streaming through his windows. Pat and Sara were still asleep. Softly, he opened his curtains, and looked out. It was a lovely clear morning, and he could see right across Greendale to the far hills. He just couldn't wait for Pat to waken up. He opened the telescope carefully, and poked it out of the open window.

At first, everything was fuzzy. Then Julian remembered that Pat had shown him how to move the tubes of the telescope until the picture became sharp and clear. Oh, how wonderful it was! He could see the cows and sheep on the hills. Rabbits coming out of their burrows, to sniff at the morning air, and nibble the grass. A horse drinking from its trough at Greendale Farm. There was the milk-tanker coming along the valley road. Far away things looked so near. It was as though everything had been painted afresh that morning, with a magic brush filled with light.

Who was that, coming along the road on a bike? It must be Miss Hubbard. Where was she off to, so early? And there was Peter Fogg's tractor just starting up, ready to begin ploughing the top field.

Julian moved the telescope round to look all the way up the valley. He looked at the tops of the high hills, where the buzzards flew. He looked at the church tower to see if he could see the time on the clock.

Pat and Sara were still asleep. It must be very early. Pat said last night that they would be able to see Ted Glen from the top of the hill. If only they would waken! Never mind, there were plenty of other things to be seen.

Julian turned the telescope again; now he found Granny Dryden's cottage. There was a twist of smoke coming out of the chimney. She must be up. Better still, there she was, coming out into the garden. Where was she off to? She went out of the garden gate, then turned into the field. She went slowly along by the hedge. Whatever was she doing? She kept close to the hedge, and seemed to be looking at something very carefully, and she was carrying something over her arm. But it was too far away for Julian to see what it was. Then he guessed.

"I know," said Julian. "Blackberries! She's picking blackberries, and that's her basket on her arm."

Then he saw something else. At the top of the field, behind some trees, where Granny Dryden couldn't see, Colonel Forbes was opening the gate. He was letting something into the field. Was it a cow? Just one cow on its own? Where were all the other cows? Colonel Forbes had thirty or more. Could it be the bull? It must be! Oh, help, what would happen if the bull saw Granny Dryden? She could never run to the gate in time to get away. She had moved a long way along the hedge now; a long way from the gate. Julian was frightened. Quickly, he put the telescope down, and ran to waken Pat and Sara.

"Quick!" shouted Julian. "Quick! Send a rocket up! Get the lifeboat out! Waken up! Mum! Dad! The bull's going to get Miss Hubbard! Waken up!"

What a fright it was for Pat and Sara. They tumbled out of bed half awake, rubbing their eyes.

"What . . . oh . . . rockets . . . ?" said Pat.

"What in all the nation . . . ?" said Sara.

"Granny Dryden . . . the bull . . . blackberries . . . " shouted Julian. He was in such a rush to tell them, that his words were all mixed up.

At last, they woke up properly. "Now then," said Pat, "take your time, and tell us the right way round. What's all this about a rocket and Granny Dryden?"

Julian took a deep breath and told them all that he had seen.

"I'd better get a move on," said Pat. "That bull's really dangerous."

He didn't even stop to get dressed! He ran out to his van in his pyjamas, and was off up the road, before Sara could get the kettle on. Julian went back to the window with the telescope, and he followed Pat's van all the way along the road. He told Sara what was happening.

"He's got to the crossroads . . . he has to wait for the tanker . . . he's turning now . . . won't be long. No, the bull hasn't seen Granny Dryden yet, but she's gone a lot further up the field, and she's getting nearer to it. It looks quiet. It's having a drink . . . now it's looking over the hedge at the cows. There's Dad, just going past the church, and the Reverend's waving to him."

Sara wrapped a blanket round Julian to keep him warm. He kept his eye to the telescope.

"Dad's going up the windy lane now; not far to go . . . he's turning by the signpost . . . he's slowing down for some sheep on the road . . . nearly there . . . yes, he's parking the van by the field gate. He's waving to Granny Dryden, but she hasn't seen him."

"He'll not be able to shout," said Sara, "because the bull would hear."

"He's in the field, now."

"What's the bull doing?" said Sara.

"Eating grass," said Julian. "It hasn't seen them . . . well, I don't think so. Dad's walking up to Granny Dryden. She's holding the basket of blackberries to show him. He's talking to her . . . taking her arm . . . yes, she's following him to the gate. The bull's looking. Has it heard them? It's walking round the trees. Come on, Dad, get a move on."

"What's it doing now?" said Sara.

"It's all right," said Julian. "They've got to the gate, and the bull's just watching them from the top of the hill. Dad's shut the gate, and they're getting into the van."

"I'll get that tea made," said Sara. "He'll be wanting a sup, after all that."

Julian followed Pat's van all the way back home. There was a good pot of tea and a good breakfast on the table by the time Pat was coming through the door.

"I saw you," said Julian, "through the telescope."

"I bet you didn't hear Granny Dryden laughing, though," said Pat. "She laughed her socks off, seeing me out in my pyjamas!"

"It's a good thing you had a clean pair on," said Sara.

"And what a good thing young Julian spotted that bull," said Pat.

"Like Great Grandad," said Julian, "rescuing sailors."

"But you rescue grannies," said Sara, "and that's every bit as good."

"I wonder," said Julian, "what we'll get out of that box next?"

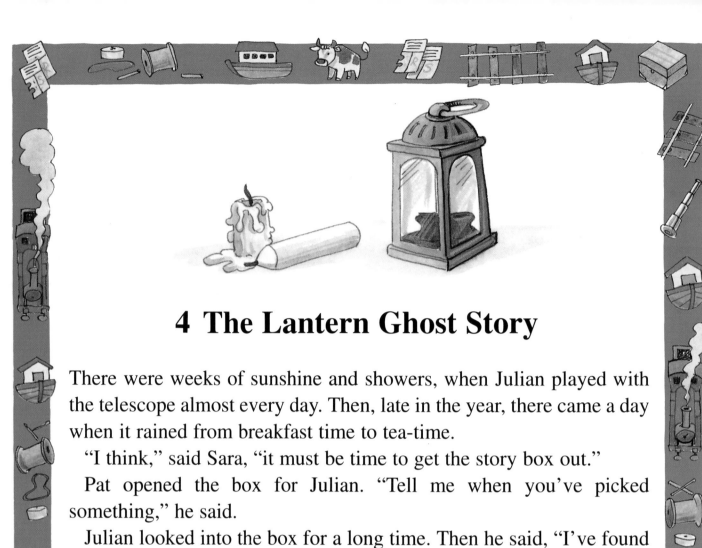

4 The Lantern Ghost Story

There were weeks of sunshine and showers, when Julian played with the telescope almost every day. Then, late in the year, there came a day when it rained from breakfast time to tea-time.

"I think," said Sara, "it must be time to get the story box out."

Pat opened the box for Julian. "Tell me when you've picked something," he said.

Julian looked into the box for a long time. Then he said, "I've found a little house, with glass walls."

"That's a house for a fire," said Sara.

"A fire?"

"A fire that makes a light," said Pat. "A candle . . . well, two candles in this one."

"But candles burn," said Sara, "so you have to be careful."

"Safety first," said Pat.

"What is it for?"

"It's a lantern," said Pat. "A light for a dark night, or a dark morning."

"But we have a torch, with a big battery," said Julian.

"They didn't have them in the old days," said Pat. "They had candles instead."

"In a glass house?" said Julian.

"To keep the wind out," said Sara.

"Because . . ."

" . . . the wind blows candles out!"

"Was it Grandad's lantern?" said Julian.

"No," said Pat. "It was *his* grandad's; your *Great-Great-Grandad*, Tom."

"Is there a story about it?"

"More than one," said Pat. "There were no electric lights in Tom's time, and no gaslights either. They only had candles, or the light of the flames when they sat and told stories by the fire on winter nights."

"Let's try it," said Julian.

Pat brought some candles from the kitchen, and fitted them into the lantern. Sara brought some matches, and lit the candles for Julian. Pat closed the little door of the lantern, and they could see the candles glowing inside.

"Let's put the electric lights out," said Sara.

The candle-flames grew bigger and brighter in the darkening room. Soft beams of light shone through the windows of the old lantern.

"Dark before tea-time," said Sara.

"Can we have the story now?" said Julian.

"There's just about time before tea," said Sara.

"If you could see all the things that old lantern has lit up," said Pat, "you would see some stories, you surely would. I'll tell you one Tom used to tell. When he was a boy he was always up to mischief; he loved playing tricks on people. Well, there was this particular story . . . people used to say there was a ghost in the Old Mill House. It was an empty ruin, even then. Tom thought he would play a trick on some of the girls at school. Young Mary Pottage and Jeannie Dryden were always teasing him. They said he was scared of ghosts. He said there were no ghosts. So they dared him to go to the Old Mill House at night, round about Hallowe'en.

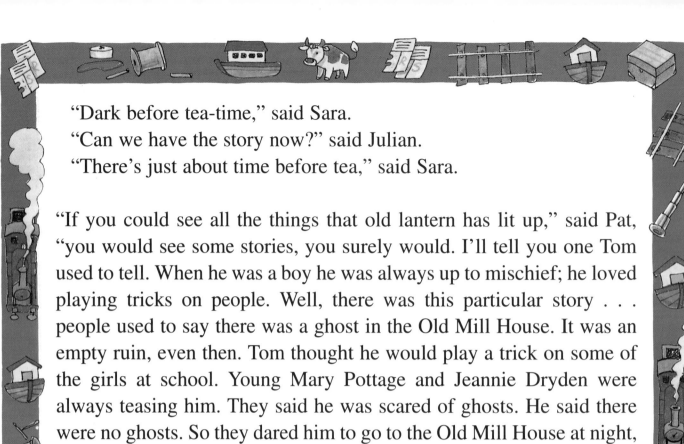

Tom borrowed his dad's lantern, even though children weren't usually allowed to use them, and set out in good time, to be there before the girls. It was a dark night, and he covered the lantern up, leaving only a small chink of light so that he could find his way.

When he got to the mill, he climbed inside and set the lantern up where its light could be seen from the road. He arranged some branches so that they would make spooky shadows on the wall. There was a bit of wind, and that made the flames flicker, so it was still more spooky. He heard the girls a long time before they got to the mill, because they were laughing and giggling so much. They had brought a candle in a jar, but the wind blew it out, so now they were feeling their way along in the darkness. Jeannie walked into a stream in the dark, and got her feet wet, and that made them giggle all the more.

Tom covered the lantern up again. Then he waited until the girls were near to the mill. He heard Mary say, "That Tom, he'll never come in this dark. He's too scared!"

He uncovered the lantern, letting the light shine on the wall. The girls were so near that he held his breath, for fear they would hear him. He could hear them both go, 'Oooooooh!'

Then Jeannie said, "*Look!*"

Tom reached out for the lantern, and began to wave it about to make the shadows move in a ghostly manner. Then he lost his footing on the loose stones, and dropped it with a great clatter!

Mary screamed, "It's the ghosts! They're after us!"

The next thing, they were both running back along the road in the dark, stumbling and stepping in puddles and muddy patches, and getting their stockings torn by the roadside brambles.

Tom shouted after them, "It's all right! It's only Tom, with the old lantern!"

But they were already too far away to hear, or too much in a panic to listen. It took Tom ages to find the lantern in the dark, scrabbling about amongst the stones, and he could not get it lit again. He had to stumble home in the pitch darkness, so he was muddy and scratched, too, by the end of the adventure.

Oh, what a telling-off they all had when they got home! They were sent early to bed with no supper; but Tom said it was worth it. Never again did the girls tease him about being scared of ghosts.

When bed-time came, Julian asked Pat if he could go to bed by lantern-light.

"And which story shall we have?" said Pat. "Shall we have *The Greendale Ghost?*"

But Julian said, "Let's have *Winnie the Pooh*, tonight. It's more cheerful."

5 A Moonlight Post

Pat was always up early, ready to deliver his letters before breakfast. In winter time, he was up so early that it was still dark outside. Then he had to take his big torch with him, so that he could see the addresses on the letters. The next morning, Julian woke up when he heard Pat's alarm-clock. Even though the sun was not up, there was a light shining on the bedroom curtains. Julian went to look out of the window. The full moon looked in at him, shining its strange light on to the garden.

"It looks like time for a moonlight post," said Pat. "Now then, what are you doing awake so early?"

"I was dreaming about the lantern," said Julian. "I dreamed that I was coming with you on the post, with the lantern shining in the dark. I held it so that you could see your letters. But . . . I wouldn't be allowed would I?"

"Well, you're not really allowed to travel in the van, but . . ."

"What, Dad!"

"If I took the post-bus. . ."

"Then I could come?"

"Yes."

"And bring the lantern?"

"If you promise to be very *very* careful, and do just as I say."

"I promise. But the post-bus never goes on the early run, so it won't be dark."

"It will do tomorrow," said Pat, smiling. "The van's going in for its service. George's picking it up tonight. So . . . "

"I can come on a moonlight post?"

"Yes, if you can waken up in time, and if there's a moon."

"You bet I can."

Julian was almost too excited to go to sleep at all that night, but Sara said, "There's no going on any moonlight trips if you don't go to sleep."

So, after two bed-time stories, Julian closed his eyes and pretended to go to sleep. He did it so well that Sara really thought he was asleep. And, in a few minutes more, he truly was, and dreaming about his moonlight expedition.

When morning came, Julian almost missed wakening up in time. He never heard Pat's alarm. But, somehow, Pat dropped his keys, just as he came into Julian's room. The jingling sound was so much like a bell, that he awoke at once.

"Is it time to go?" was the first thing he said.

"It's all right," said Pat. "There's plenty of time for breakfast."

Julian looked out of the window. The moon was shining, but there were a good many black clouds in the sky, and a wind blowing. As the clouds flew across the sky, they covered the moon up, bringing deep darkness back to the earth.

"We're going to need that lantern," said Pat.

They had a good breakfast, and Julian took Sara her breakfast in bed.

"That's lovely," she said. "Now you will behave yourself, won't you, and do as you're told?"

"Promise, promise, promise," said Julian, giving her a bigger kiss than usual.

"Good lad."

"Guess what?" said Pat. "The battery in my torch has gone flat, and I have no spares."

"It's a good thing Julian's bringing the lantern, then," said Sara. "You'd be lost without him."

"I would, an' all," said Pat. "Come on, Julian, it's time we were off."

Julian put some spare candles in his pocket, Pat lit the lantern, and they were off.

It was strange and magical being out in the morning moonlight, and in the post-bus as well. Greendale was beginning to come to life, even though it was so early. There were lights in the cow shed at Greendale Farm, and the sound of a tractor starting, somewhere up in the hills.

As the post-bus wound its way along the country roads, they saw things you would never see in the day time. Many a rabbit froze in the beams of the headlights. They saw a stoat crossing the road by Greendale Farm, and a fox raced across the road at the cross roads on the way to Thompson Ground. There was a huge owl in a tree by the church. When Julian went to deliver the Reverend's letters, it flew out of the tree, making a loud whoooooooo sound. Julian almost dropped the lantern! He had heard owls many a time before, but never so close.

When the moon was shining clear, Pat could see the addresses by moonlight; but, when clouds covered the moon, Julian held the lantern close to the envelopes so that Pat could see.

"That's a really good help, young Julian," said Pat. "I don't know what I would have done if you hadn't woken up in time."

Then Julian shone the lantern on the pathways; there was many a tricky tree-root or loose stone that you could fall over.

When they arrived at Granny Dryden's cottage, Julian was surprised to see that she was up and about.

"I get up a long time before the lark," she said, "and I have the kettle on. Will you have a sup of tea?"

"Thank you very much," said Pat. "It's a chilly morning."

They sat by a good log fire, and warmed their hands on their mugs of tea. How cosy it was, sitting there in the early morning, when most people were still in bed.

When they went out again, there was another surprise for Julian. There was a new light in the sky; a yellow glow spreading at the edges of darkness, where the sky met the line of the hills far across the valley.

"Here comes the sun," said Pat

"Oh . . . oh!" said Julian. He looked sad. The light of his lantern would not be needed for long now. Its brightness was fading already. The moon, too, looked faint. The light at the edge of the sky grew stronger; it changed from yellow to gold, and crept higher above the hills. The clouds filled the sky, and it was darker for a time. Then the sun came up, lighting the clouds like a huge fire, and spreading its glow across the fields. Julian blew his lantern out.

"Never mind," said Pat. "We'll have another breakfast when we get home, and there'll be more times when we can take the lantern out in the dark."

Pat and Julian were cheerful as they travelled home along the valley. The sun made a lovely light, coming low across the grass, and through the branches of the trees. The moon looked down at them between gaps in the clouds, very faint now, sharing the sky with the great sun. All the letters and parcels had been safely delivered, and Julian felt hungry enough for *two* more breakfasts.

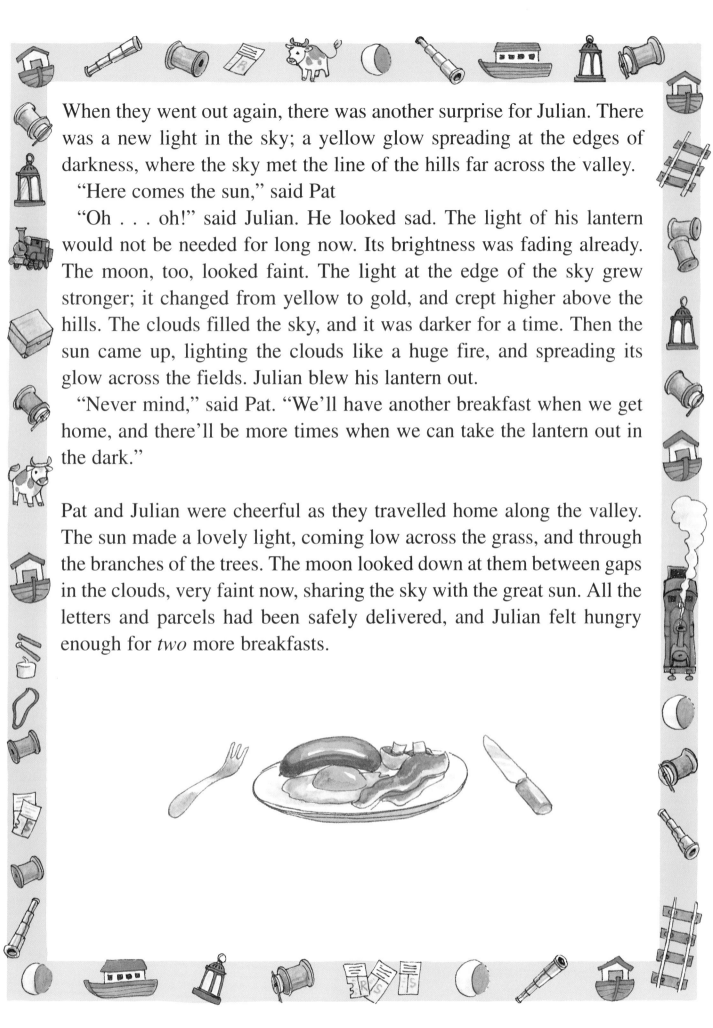

6 A Bag of Bobbins

When Pat called at the Post Office for the letters one Saturday morning, Mrs Goggins said, "I've been collecting bobbins up for years, and I wondered if the children would like them to play with?" She gave Pat a big plastic bag full of empty cotton-reels.

"Bobbins?" said Pat. "We played with them for hours, when I was a lad. Thank you very much. They'll be just the thing for a rainy day. I'll give them out as I go along. Special delivery. Thanks very much. Cheerio!"

"Bye, Pat!"

Jess was the first one to play with the bobbins. He could not guess what they were, when Pat put them down in the back of the van. Were they a new kind of fish? He kept a close watch on them all the way along the windy roads to Greendale Farm. They rolled about with each turn of the road, and seemed to be alive. Then one of them rolled out of the bag. It came fast across the floor towards Jess. A mouse! It must be a mouse! A new kind of mouse, that could run without any legs!

Jess jumped on the bobbin. He batted it with his paw. Away it went, whizzing across the floor, to be lost behind a sack of letters. He stalked it. He crept closer and closer. Then he pounced. Caught it! It lay still between his paws. It must be dead. Now he would eat it. Oh, how it hurt his teeth! Poor Jess! He batted the bobbin away again, and it ran and hid behind another sack. It must not be dead after all. He watched it for a long time. It never moved again.

When Pat stopped at Greendale Farm, he said, "Whatever are you doing, Jess? These bobbins are not for cats; they are for the children to play with. Never mind, you can have that one, now you've given it a good chewing."

At all the places Pat called that day, if they had children, he left a pocketful of bobbins for them, with the letters. What a surprise they had when they came home from school. He kept a good pocketful for Julian.

Sara said, "When I was a girl we used to do French knitting with bobbins. We made all sorts of things."

"And we used to make bobbin-tractors," said Pat. "We had races, me, Ted, and Charlie. And, do you know, Charlie was a real champion. He nearly always won."

"Who was Charlie?" said Sara, laughing.

"The Reverend, of course! Well, that's what we called him then."

"Oh," said Sara; "I never think of him now as Charlie."

"Well, it was a long time before he thought of being a Reverend. He was just Charlie to us. And . . . I wouldn't mind making a bobbin-tractor now, if only I could remember how to do it."

"You'll be having races again, with Ted and Charlie," said Sara.

"I wouldn't be at all surprised," said Pat. "Now, I wonder if I have one anywhere, from when I was a lad. I'll just have a look in that old story box."

7 A Small Contraption

When Julian came home from school, Pat was lying flat on the floor, looking for something under the sofa, and holding Jess tightly by the collar.

"Whatever are you doing, Dad?" he said.

A muffled voice answered; it didn't sound like Pat at all.

"Looking for my bobbin-tractor."

"Your bobbin-*what?*"

"My . . . oh, hello Julian . . . home from school?" Pat sat up. He looked dizzy. His hair was ruffled. He was covered in bits of fluff from the carpet.

"What are you doing?"

"I told you," said Pat. "Looking for . . ."

" . . . a *tractor?* Under the settee?"

"A bobbin-tractor. It's only so big. See if you can get it. You're so small, you can reach further than me. I'll keep hold of Jess."

Julian was still puzzled. "Mum!" he shouted. "Has Dad gone bonkers?"

Sara came in from the garage.

"No, love, it's just the bobbins," said Sara.

"Don't you start!" said Julian.

"Sorry, but you see . . ."

And she told him all about Mrs Goggins and the bobbins, and the bobbin-tractors that Pat used to race when he was a boy, and how he had found one in the story box, and it had got stuck under the settee.

"And why does Jess want it?" said Julian, still puzzled.

"He wants to kill it," said Sara. "And I can't blame him."

"Got it!" shouted Pat.

He came out from underneath the settee with a small object in his hand, that whirred feebly, like a tired beetle. "Now, then, watch this," he said, "when I wind it up. Can you hold Jess?"

He had a small contraption that seemed to be made of matchsticks, elastic-bands, bits of sliced candle, and a bobbin.

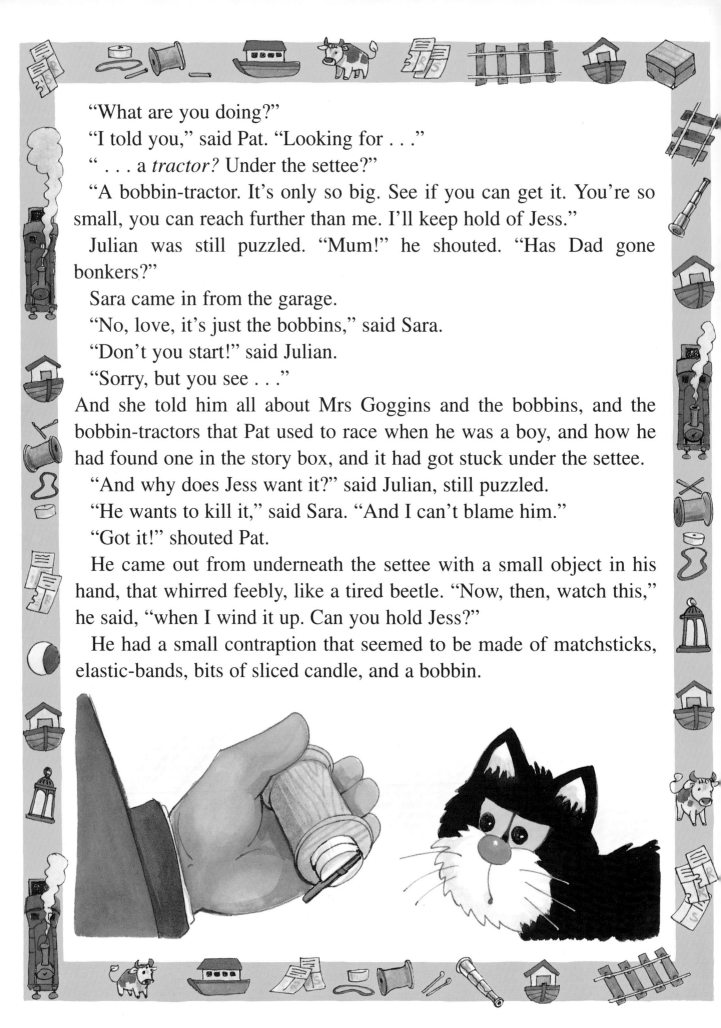

"Watch the mess that's waiting to be cleaned up in that kitchen," said Sara.

"I'll clear it up in a minute," said Pat. "But watch!"

He put the thing down on the carpet. It set off again, climbing over lumps in the carpet, then over an upturned saucer, just like a little tractor.

"Did *you* make that?" said Julian.

"Yes."

"Will you show me how?"

"I certainly will!"

"Help!" said Sara.

"We won't make a mess, mum, honest," said Julian.

Just then, Jess pulled away from Julian's grip. He pounced on the tractor, and killed it.

"We'll have to make another one, now," said Julian.

"Only," said Sara, "when you've tidied up, had a wash, and had your tea."

8 Tractors Galore!

It was almost bed-time. Jess was shut in the kitchen. Sara was sitting in the chair reading her book. Pat and Julian had made a big newspaper-island, to keep the carpet clean. All round them were bobbin-tractors, creeping here and there across the newspaper-fields. They had built all kinds of obstacles for them to climb over, or under, or through. There were cereal-packet tunnels; clay mountains; deserts made of rice. There was even a water-splash, in a biscuit-tin lid, but that was trying to leak away. Sara had *not* noticed that. All of a sudden, she looked up from her book and said, "Bed-time."

"Oh, no!" said Julian.

"I think it is," said Pat. "Ten minutes to clear up?"

"Five," said Sara.

"But there will be time for a story?" said Julian.

"There always is," said Pat.

"Yes," said Sara.

"That's right. If you're quick."

They were quick, and, when all the tractors were safe in their biscuit-tin on the bedside table, Julian said, "Tell me the story of the bobbins."

"It begins," said Pat, "long long ago, when bobbins were first made in Greendale. When great-great Uncle George had a piece of coppice woodland to grow the wood, and a hand-lathe in the back of his cottage to make the bobbins."

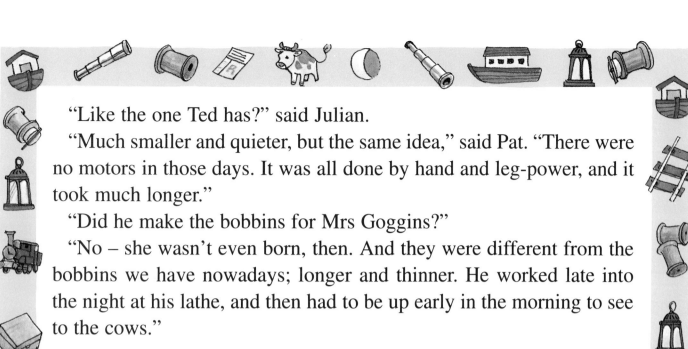

"Like the one Ted has?" said Julian.

"Much smaller and quieter, but the same idea," said Pat. "There were no motors in those days. It was all done by hand and leg-power, and it took much longer."

"Did he make the bobbins for Mrs Goggins?"

"No – she wasn't even born, then. And they were different from the bobbins we have nowadays; longer and thinner. He worked late into the night at his lathe, and then had to be up early in the morning to see to the cows."

"Did he have a farm as well?"

"Oh, yes. He had to do both jobs, just to get enough to eat. When he had made enough bobbins, he would set out on his horse, to ride to Pencaster to sell them to the thread merchants. It was a long, cold, and hungry journey, but he could get food in the town to bring back to the lonely cottage on the moors. As winter came on, and the snow came, he could not get into Pencaster. So he changed his lathe to make something different. He made little wooden trees, and wooden men and women, and pegs and counters."

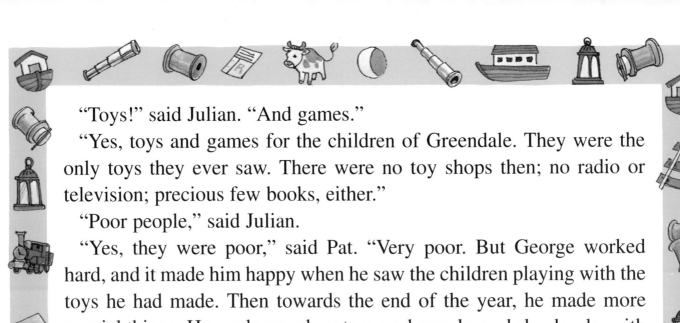

"Toys!" said Julian. "And games."

"Yes, toys and games for the children of Greendale. They were the only toys they ever saw. There were no toy shops then; no radio or television; precious few books, either."

"Poor people," said Julian.

"Yes, they were poor," said Pat. "Very poor. But George worked hard, and it made him happy when he saw the children playing with the toys he had made. Then towards the end of the year, he made more special things. He made wooden stars, and angels, and shepherds, with their sheep. Not on his lathe. He sat by the fire in the winter darkness, and carved the softer wood that was the wrong shape to be made into bobbins. He showed his wife how to do it, too, and she helped when she could spare the time. Can you guess what they were making, then?"

"Things for Christmas?"

"Yes, Christmas Tree decorations, and all the valley loved him for his kindness."

"Is that the end of the story?" said Julian, looking sleepy.

"It is the end of the first part," said Pat. "But I'll tell you more tomorrow, and I will show you something that great-great Uncle George made."

A moment later, Julian was asleep.

9 A Cold Christmas

It was a good thing that the next day was a Sunday, because Julian wanted to hear the second part of the story the moment he woke up. Perhaps he had been dreaming about that long-ago maker of toys and bobbins. Whatever the reason, he woke Pat and Sara far too early, and there would be no peace until Pat finished the story.

When Pat had made a cup of tea, and taken a pot for Sara, he went to get the story box.

"Well," Pat began, "I told you about great-great Uncle George, and the wonderful toys he made, as well as making bobbins through long days and nights."

"And," said Julian, "you said you would show me something that he made."

"I will," said Pat. "Something in the story box. Something you have not seen, yet. It was one very cold Christmas. It had been a hard year in every way. The weather was bad, the crops were scarce and the cows were thin and poor in their yield of milk. Many families went hungry, but there was not much that George could do about that. What he could do was to keep on making his wooden toys, even when he was tired, so that there would be something for the children to look forward to at Christmas. Then, he heard of one family who were in great distress. The father had died, and there were young children to be cared for and fed. The neighbours helped as much as they could, giving them a share

of their own food, so that they did not starve. But what could they look forward to at Christmas? Not much."

"Poor things," said Julian, looking sad.

"But," said Pat, "George decided to do something special for them. He would make them the best toy he had ever made in his life. He made them . . ."

"A bobbin tractor!" said Julian.

"Not a bobbin-tractor," said Pat. "but . . . *this*!" Pat opened the story box, lifted out a package that Julian had not seen before, and said, "Open it carefully, and see if you know what it is."

"Oh," said Julian. It looked like a large boat, with a house on it, filled with wooden animals. "It's a . . . you know . . . like the one in that story in the Bible!"

"An ark," said Pat. "A Noah's ark, with all the animals, carved and painted in his best pieces of wood, that George had been saving up for years and years, for just such a special time as this. And it certainly was the finest toy he ever made."

"For the poor family with no dad," said Julian.

"Yes," said Pat.

"And tell him," said Sara, coming in with hot milk for Julian, "what happened afterwards."

"The children had a wonderful time, playing with that ark and all the animals in it, but they almost lost it," said Pat. "A rare thing happened for Greendale at that time. A man came riding his horse along the turnpike road from Pencaster. He said he had come from people in Manchester who had collected money to feed the poorest people in the countryside. The good Greendale folk told him to call at the cottage of the family with no father. He gave them money to help them, but then he saw the wonderful wooden ark that the children were playing with. He said he would give them more money if they would sell him the ark."

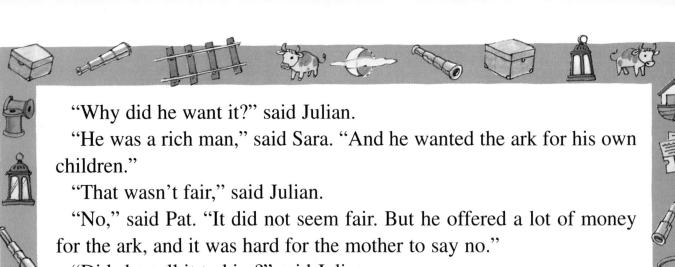

"Why did he want it?" said Julian.

"He was a rich man," said Sara. "And he wanted the ark for his own children."

"That wasn't fair," said Julian.

"No," said Pat. "It did not seem fair. But he offered a lot of money for the ark, and it was hard for the mother to say no."

"Did she sell it to him?" said Julian.

"She nearly did. You see, the extra money would mean they could have shoes as well as something to eat, and they might even be able to go to school. But they had another stroke of luck. Great-great Uncle George heard about all this before the rich man rode away, and before he paid for the ark. He told the poor mother to sell her ark to the rich man, and he would make another ark for her children, and it would be even better than the first one. So that is what they did. The second ark was still more splendid, and the extra money bought them shoes and food for the whole year. After that, they had good luck and did well in life."

"But how did the ark get into our story box?" said Julian. "And which one is it?"

"The true answer," said Sara, "is that no one really knows."

"But," said Pat, "it is not the end of the story. The rich man's friends in Manchester admired the wonderful ark he had brought back for his children from Greendale. They wanted such a wonderful toy for their own children. They pestered him until he told them where he had bought it. So, it wasn't long before another man rode into Greendale, asking to see the man who had made the wonderful ark. And that is how George became a famous toy-maker, and, after some years, a rich man himself, with a fine house in Pencaster. But he never forgot the time when he was a poor maker of bobbins. To help him to remember, he had a sign made to hang outside his shop in the town. It showed an ark, with the animals climbing on board, and Noah waving them on. In the sky, instead of a rainbow, there was a great arch made of . . . ?"

"Bobbins!" said Julian.

"That's right," said Pat. "And that *is* the end of the story. Except for the mystery of how that ark came to be in our story box. Whenever I asked my grandad, he said, 'I will tell you one day.' But he never did. So we will never know. I expect it was a present from great-great uncle George."

"Or his son, Arthur," said Sara.

"You never know," said Pat.

Julian played with the ark all that day, and for many a day afterwards. One day, he asked Sara if he could send it out to sea, floating in the garden-pond.

"Oh, no," said Sara. "I don't think it will float. It is so very old, I'm sure it would soon sink, and the paint might not be waterproof. I have another idea, though. We could make another ark, just like the old one."

Sara helped Julian to get wood and paints, glue, nails, and all the things needed to make an ark. Julian made animals to go in their ark; copies of all the animals in Greendale. There were farm animals, like the sheep, the cows, a massive Charolais bull, and a black and white cat just like Jess. There were wild animals; badgers, rabbits, foxes, stoats, magpies, and crows. They painted the new ark in waterproof paints, all the colours of the rainbow, and Katy and Tom came to see it set sail across the garden pond.

As the years went by, Julian told many a story about the new ark, and its adventures when Greendale was flooded, but he never forgot the story of the first ark that great-great Uncle George made, such a long time ago.

10 The Great Greendale Bobbin Race

On Monday, Julian took his best bobbin-tractor to school. He also took a pocketful of bobbins, just in case there were any children who had not had bobbins delivered by Pat. He felt sure that Mr Pringle would like to see how the bobbin-tractor could go, and he might want to make one for himself.

"Wonderful!" said Mr Pringle. "Just the thing for our design and technology work. Do please put it on the interest table, Julian. Thank you for bringing it."

"Please, Mr Pringle, what's design and tech-wotsit?" said Tom Pottage.

"Playing with bobbins," said Mr Pringle.

"Great!" said Tom.

"And," said Mr Pringle, "Julian has brought some spare bobbins . . ."

He didn't get a chance to finish. Everybody in the class had brought a bobbin-tractor out of his or her school-bag, and was waving it at Mr Pringle.

"All quiet, now, please!" called Mr Pringle. "We must take the register."

As Mr Pringle called the names, and collected the dinner-money, bobbin-tractors began creeping about all over the room. And then, when it was time to get the maths books out, someone stepped on little Sara Gilbertson's bobbin-tractor, and she burst into tears. Tom Pottage said he would help her to make a new one at play-time, so she soon cheered up.

"That's very kind, Tom," said Mr Pringle. "But we must have all the bobbin-tractors on the Interest Table, now, please. Then, for art, we'll get the paints out, and paint them." The children all cheered.

"And," Mr Pringle went on, "as Julian has brought lots more bobbins, everyone can make another tractor."

"Mine's not a tractor, it's a tank," said Bill Thompson.

"Mine's a combine," said Katy.

"Can we have races?" said Tom.

"Why not?" said Mr Pringle. "A splendid idea."

"Mine's a doctor's car," said Sara Gilbertson.

"Whatever they are," said Mr Pringle, "you will be able to decorate them and play with them after break."

"Are you going to make one, Mr Pringle?" said Julian.

"I certainly am," said Mr Pringle, "but I don't suppose it will win any races."

Once the maths was done, it was bobbin-tractors all day at Greendale School. They built a tractor-world out of boxes and green paper from the stock-cupboard, complete with hills for the tractors to climb, and barns to keep them in at night. They had races and hill-climbing competitions, and there was a seaside tractor place, made from sand and clay, in the sand-tray. Some tractors even turned into engines for boats, with the fitting of paddle-wheels, and went chugging round the water-tray. There was no end to what could be done with them. When Pat came in with the letters, he was sent off to the Post Office to see if Mrs Goggins had any more bobbins to spare. Mr Pringle had to send an urgent order to the Education Office for more elastic bands. They never did guess what they were wanted for.

When home-time came, Mr Pringle said they could take one tractor home each, and leave one at school.

Then the grown-ups started making bobbin-tractors.

At the Post Office, Mrs Goggins sold out of packets of elastic bands. She gave away the last of her empty bobbins. Then she sold out of reels of cotton. Drawers and cupboards all over Greendale were ransacked for any old bobbins that might be tucked away.

When the Church's Christmas Fête came round, the Reverend Timms announced that there would be a Grand Greendale Bobbin-Tractor Race. Entry 50 pence per tractor, with Dorothy Thompson's delicious fruit pies as the prizes. There were speed races and distance races, and anyone could enter.

Ted Glen made a double-sized bobbin on his lathe, then built a giant tractor with it. He was disqualified from the races, but the Reverend gave him a prize for originality.

Katy and Tom made a tandem-tractor, with two bobbins joined together. It got stuck at the side of the track, but they had to have a prize for originality as well.

In a straight race, with standard tractors only, the Reverend won by six lengths.
    "The Lord guided my bobbin," he said. "It's no credit to me."
    "Ooh, I don't know about that," said Pat. "You used to win when we were lads, long before you were a Reverend."

Pat made a Post Office tractor. It lost its race because it, too, got stuck half way along the track.
    "It's stopped," said Julian, "to collect the letters."

It was a long time before the bobbin-tractor craze died down in Greendale; every year after that, there was a bobbin season around the end of November, and Greendale School had top marks in all the county for science and design.

11 The Greendale Light Railway

"Mum! There are some old tickets in the story box," said Julian. "It says: GREENDALE LIGHT RAILWAY COMPANY on them, but there are no trains in Greendale!"

"There are no trains now," said Sara, "but that doesn't mean there never have been any."

"Is there a story about these tickets?" said Julian.

"There surely is," said Sara. "But you'll have to wait for Dad to finish his letters if you want to hear it."

"Why? Can't you tell me?"

"I could, but I won't, because it really is Pat's story. You see, he put those tickets in the story box. He was the one who bought them, and he was the one who was there when part of the story happened."

"I can't wait," said Julian.

"You'll have to," said Sara.

And that was that.

When Pat came home, Julian was waiting for him. He hadn't even got his coat off before Julian was at his elbow, saying, "Dad, Dad, tell me about the Greendale Light Railway!"

"Hang on," said Pat. "Give me time to make a cup of tea, and get Jess some milk."

"You'll have no peace till you tell him," said Sara. "He's been

48

pestering me ever since he came home from school."

"Well, I'm glad you saved it for me to tell," said Pat.

When Pat had got his slippers on, and a good pot of tea at his side, he said, "Now, then, about this railway . . . A long time ago, it was a quarry-railway, and it went all the way up Greendale, right to the top of the valley, where they used to get the lovely Greendale stone. They used the railway to bring the stone down to Pencaster."

"Could people ride on the train?" said Julian.

"No," said Pat, "but letters and parcels could. There was a guard's van at the end, and they used to put the post in there."

"Where did the postman pick them up?"

"It was Postman Ron in those days," said Pat. "There was a place where the train stopped – Greendale Halt – to take on coal and water, and that was where Ron picked up the post."

"Did he have a Jess?"

"No, but he had a dog. And he had no van; he had to walk all the way up the dale with his letters, and it was good to have a dog to go with him."

"What was it called?"

"Don."

"Postman Ron and his big dog, Don!" said Julian.

"It *was* a big dog," said Pat. "An Alsatian. I can tell you; Ron never had any trouble with the farm-dogs."

"Or with robbers," said Julian.

"True," said Pat.

"He must have been a good walker," said Julian.

"He walked forty miles in a day," said Pat. "But, sometimes, he could get a lift in the guard's van, on the train, specially when the weather was bad. He could ride up to the end of the valley, and then walk back, delivering the letters as he went. But there wasn't always a train at the right time, then he had to walk it both ways. When they made proper roads up the dale, he had a bike, and Don trotted along beside him."

"It must have been hard work," said Julian.

"Very," said Pat. "But, my goodness, he was fit."

"And then," said Sara, "can you believe it? He used to go fell-racing at weekends. Running miles and miles across the hills."

"It was nothing to him," said Pat.

"Tell me about the railway," said Julian. "Which way did it go?"

"You can can still see some of the tracks," said Pat. "Would you like to see them?"

"Ooh, yes."

"Right; we'll have a walk up there tomorrow," said Pat, "and I'll show you. And then I'll tell you the rest of the story."

"I'll come as well," said Sara. "I haven't seen that old railway-track since I was a little girl, helping to drive the cows home for milking."

51

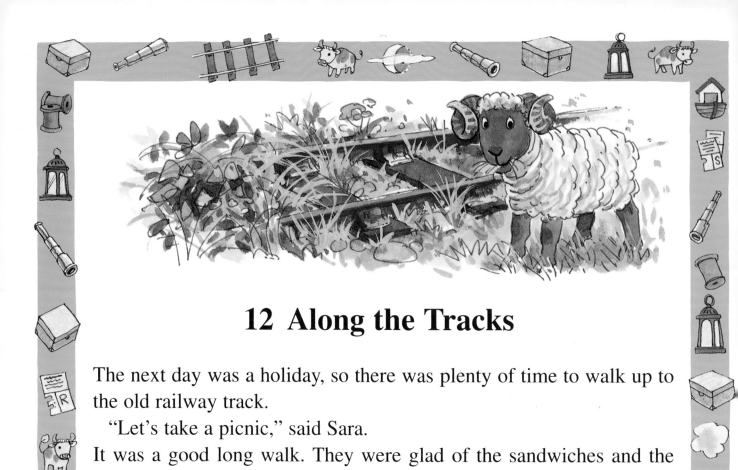

12 Along the Tracks

The next day was a holiday, so there was plenty of time to walk up to the old railway track.

"Let's take a picnic," said Sara.

It was a good long walk. They were glad of the sandwiches and the flasks of tea. They came at last to an old bridge.

"Look over there," said Pat.

They looked over the wall at the side of the bridge. There was the old track, going across the fields, through a cutting and a small wood. There were cows and sheep where the trains had once run.

"Look!" shouted Julian, "I can see some bits of the track!"

Here and there, you could see part of the old rails; but they soon disappeared into the mud and the cow pats.

"It would take some doing to get trains going up here again," said Pat.

"What happened to them?" said Julian. "Where have they gone?"

"They just used up all the stone in the quarry," said Pat. "So there was no need for the railway. Then they had the idea of making it into a railway for visitors to ride on. They bought some carriages from a railway down south somewhere, all in green and gold. They were very posh. But they didn't get enough people to ride on it, so they had to close it down."

"And Postman Ron had to walk all the way," said Julian.

"No," said Sara. "It was Postman Syd by then, and he had a motorbike, with a sidecar to carry the letters and parcels."

"So when did you buy the tickets in the story box?" said Julian.

"On the last day the Greendale line was open; the last run on the last day," said Pat. "I'll never forget it. We were all sad to see the railway closing down, but they made something of a celebration of it, for all that. They had a brass band, and stalls with cakes and ginger-beer, and the Mayor of Pencaster came and made a speech."

Just then, there was a *toot-toot!*

"Look out!" said Julian. "There's a train coming."

There was the sound of a motorbike.

"It's Postman Syd," said Sara.

"It's Peter Fogg," said Pat.

And it was. He was out for a ride, with his girl friend, Jenny.

"Now, then," said Peter. "Are you waiting for a train?"

"It'll be a long wait," said Pat.

"Nay, you'll be all right if you go down to Pencaster," said Jenny. "They've opened the riverside line today."

"She's right," said Peter. "It's that Railway Preservation Society. They've put new track down on the Pencaster section, and they've got one of the old locos working. You can have a ride for 50 pence. They're starting tomorrow."

"Can we go on it, Dad?" said Julian.

"Yes, of course we can. We're going tomorrow," said Pat, smiling. "I have the tickets in my pocket. Look!"

"Oooh, great!" said Julian. "What a lovely surprise."

"We'll take a short cut home, just for now," said Pat. "Along the old tracks."

"It'll be quite safe," said Sara. "There won't be any trains here for years."

"But let's keep together, young Julian," said Pat. "In case a sheep fancies you for its dinner. Cheerio!"

They waved goodbye to Peter and Jenny, and set out for home.

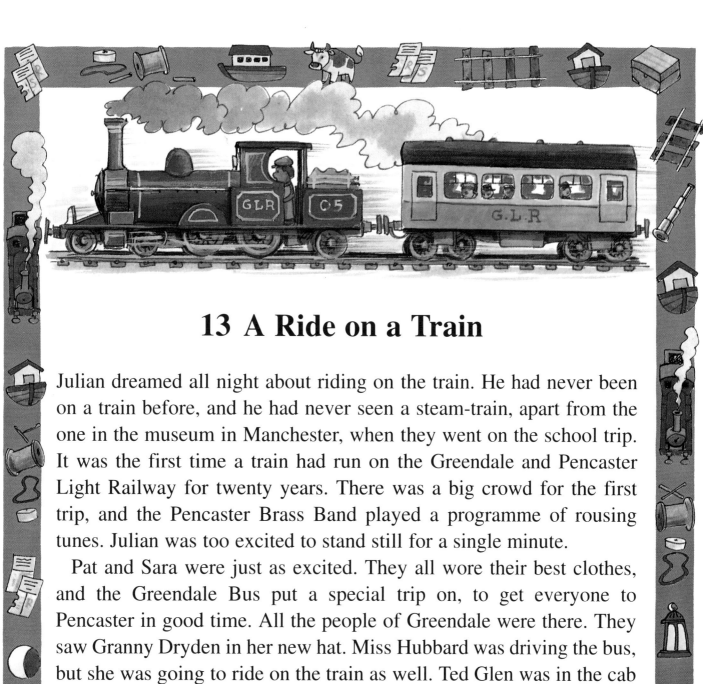

13 A Ride on a Train

Julian dreamed all night about riding on the train. He had never been on a train before, and he had never seen a steam-train, apart from the one in the museum in Manchester, when they went on the school trip. It was the first time a train had run on the Greendale and Pencaster Light Railway for twenty years. There was a big crowd for the first trip, and the Pencaster Brass Band played a programme of rousing tunes. Julian was too excited to stand still for a single minute.

Pat and Sara were just as excited. They all wore their best clothes, and the Greendale Bus put a special trip on, to get everyone to Pencaster in good time. All the people of Greendale were there. They saw Granny Dryden in her new hat. Miss Hubbard was driving the bus, but she was going to ride on the train as well. Ted Glen was in the cab of the engine, stoking up the boiler; he was going to drive the train for this first run. There was a small fair, and stalls selling burgers, and fish-and-chips, and candy-floss. There were clouds of black smoke and silvery steam from the engine. Everyone jumped when Ted pulled a rope, letting off a loud blast from the steam-whistle.

"Steam up!" he shouted.

The Mayor of Pencaster made a speech, ending, " . . . and I have pleasure in announcing the Greendale and Pencaster Light Railway well and truly open."

"Mind how you go!" said Pat.

"All aboard," said Ted.

They climbed up the high steps into the carriages. The doors went slam-slam-slam all along the length of the train, Ted gave a long blast on the whistle, and they were off.

They rumbled over the bridge, high above the river, then along by the water, on the way back towards Greendale. The wheels made a funny *chock-at-a-chock . . . chock-at-a-chock . . . chock-at-a-chock* sound as they went along. It sounded to Julian like a song. It made Pat and Sara think of times long ago when they were young.

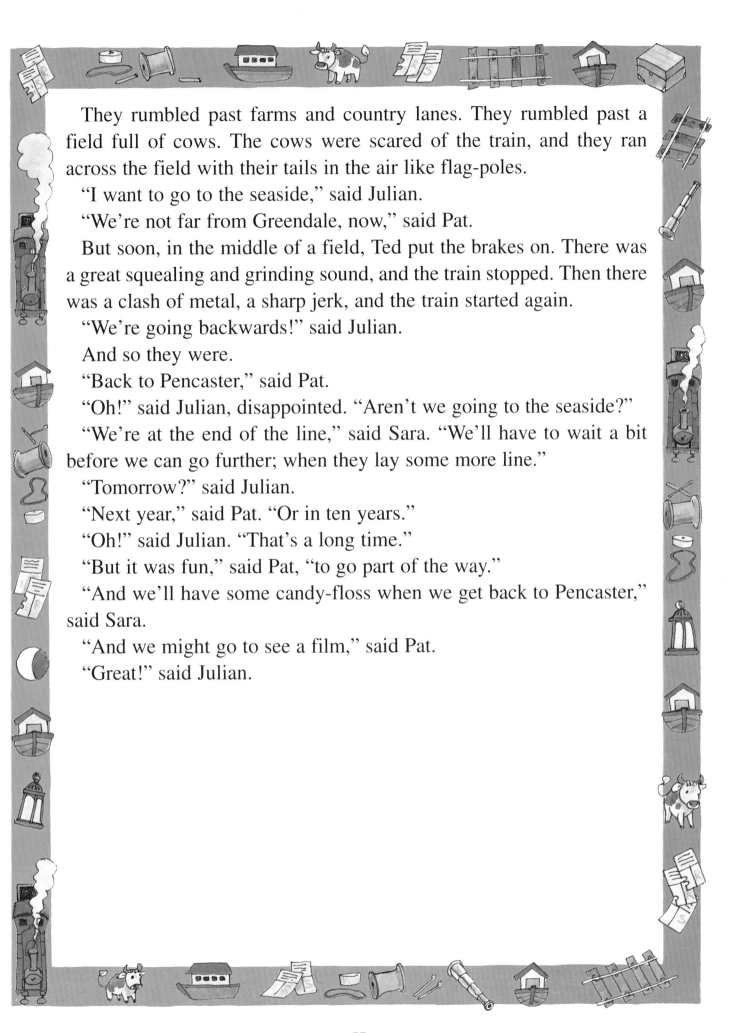

They rumbled past farms and country lanes. They rumbled past a field full of cows. The cows were scared of the train, and they ran across the field with their tails in the air like flag-poles.

"I want to go to the seaside," said Julian.

"We're not far from Greendale, now," said Pat.

But soon, in the middle of a field, Ted put the brakes on. There was a great squealing and grinding sound, and the train stopped. Then there was a clash of metal, a sharp jerk, and the train started again.

"We're going backwards!" said Julian.

And so they were.

"Back to Pencaster," said Pat.

"Oh!" said Julian, disappointed. "Aren't we going to the seaside?"

"We're at the end of the line," said Sara. "We'll have to wait a bit before we can go further; when they lay some more line."

"Tomorrow?" said Julian.

"Next year," said Pat. "Or in ten years."

"Oh!" said Julian. "That's a long time."

"But it was fun," said Pat, "to go part of the way."

"And we'll have some candy-floss when we get back to Pencaster," said Sara.

"And we might go to see a film," said Pat.

"Great!" said Julian.

14 The Newest Story

When they got home, Julian said, "Can we put our tickets in the story box?"

"There are two sets of tickets, now," said Pat. "The old ones and the new ones. We can put them all in."

"And there will be two stories to tell," said Julian.

"The old one and the new one," said Pat.

"And I'll know them both," said Julian.

"You might know more stories than we know," said Sara. "The stories that have not happened yet."

"That will be a long way away," said Julian. "Ten years or more."

But he was wrong. Only a week later, there was a big storm in Greendale. It started on the Tuesday night, with terrible wind and rain. Then, in the middle of the night the lightning began, and the thunder rolled and banged its way along the length of the valley. The lightning flashed and crackled, again and again, and Julian ran to creep under the blankets between Sara and Pat, in their big warm bed. Of all places in the world, this was the place he felt most safe.

When the daylight came, what a mess they saw outside! The wind had broken dozens of branches and twigs from the trees, and they were lying scattered all over the garden. The flowers had been broken down by the wind, and big pools of water were everywhere. The field next to the house had turned into a lake, and the ducks were having a great time, swimming and quacking and plucking at the grasses.

Pat set out to collect the letters from the village Post Office, as he did every morning. But Mrs. Goggins greeted him with a long face. "The letters haven't come today, Pat," she said. "They do say there's flooding on the road to Pencaster, but I can't get a peep out of the phone, I think the line must be down."

"Well," said Pat. "I'll go in the van and see how far I can get. At least I can find out what's happening."

"Mind how you go, Pat," said Mrs Goggins. "We don't want you getting swept away in the floods."

"No fear of that," said Pat. "I'll be careful. Cheerio!"

Pat drove along slowly, towards Pencaster. He had to watch out for big branches lying in the road. Just by Greendale Farm a tree had blown down, but Peter Fogg was already there with his tractor, clearing it away, and there was just room to get past.

Another mile or so, and, round a corner and down the hill, the road disappeared into the water. The river had burst its banks, and now it was flowing down the road.

"Well, that's that, Jess," said Pat. "There's certainly no hope of getting the letters from Pencaster across all that water. We could be stranded for a week before that lot goes down."

Pat was just turning the van round to go back to tell Mrs Goggins, when he heard – *toot toot – toot toot!*

"Bless me," said Pat. "That sounded like that steam-train!"

He wound his window down and looked out. The Pencaster and Greendale Light Railway was indeed steaming along in the pouring rain! The track ran along a high embankment, well above the level of the floods. The train had got through when nothing else could! Pat could see a light flashing from the cab. The train went along a little way, and Pat drove back along the road, keeping pace with it.

"The end of the line must be near here," said Pat.

Surely enough, the train's brakes went on, and it stopped. Pat climbed the fence into the field, and went splashing across the sopping grass, to see what was happening. Ted Glen was in the cab. He shouted to Pat, "I've got the mail! Can you come and get it?"

It was true. The letters had come by train, just as they had done, long years ago.

"Well done, Ted!" Pat shouted against the wind.

"Like a cup of tea?" said Ted.

"Tea?"

Pat couldn't believe his ears.

"Come aboard."

Pat climbed into the cab. He was glad to be out of the rain for a while, before he had to set off back across the field with the sacks of letters.

It was lovely and warm on the platform of the engine. Ted opened the fire-door, to shovel in more coal. A great warm glow came out, as the flames licked and swirled in the opening. Even with the fire-door closed, the engine was like a giant hot radiator. On a little bracket, Ted had a kettle heated by a steam-pipe, and it was boiling merrily. He brewed the tea in a pot balanced on top of the engine, and they sat with their hot mugs of tea, in the middle of the wet and windy field, as cosy as Julian had been, snuggled down in bed.

"It's a good job you got through," said Pat. "There would have been no post for days. But, how did you manage to get to Pencaster to start the train up? There must be six feet of water on that road."

"There was only one way I could go," said Ted. "I walked along the railway-tracks. I thought they'd be clear of the water, with being so high above the road. It was a grim walk, mind, but it was safe enough; I knew there would be no train coming, because I'm the only one that drives it."

"What made you think of doing that?" said Pat.

"You told me that story, once," said Ted, "about how they used to bring the post on the railway, long ago, when it was a quarry railway,

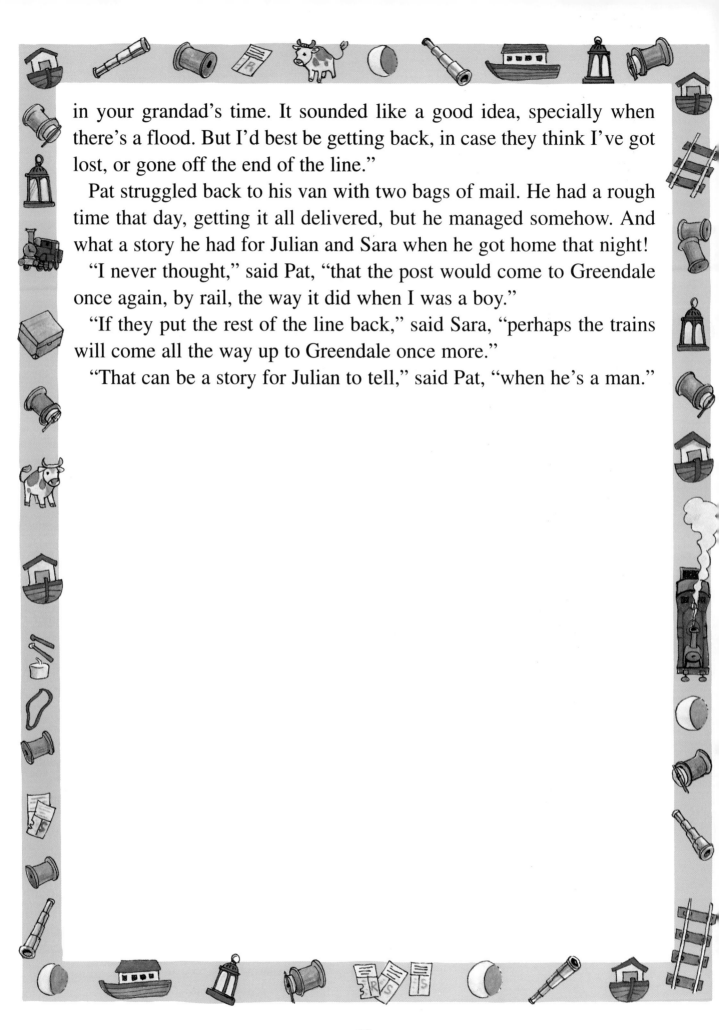

in your grandad's time. It sounded like a good idea, specially when there's a flood. But I'd best be getting back, in case they think I've got lost, or gone off the end of the line."

Pat struggled back to his van with two bags of mail. He had a rough time that day, getting it all delivered, but he managed somehow. And what a story he had for Julian and Sara when he got home that night!

"I never thought," said Pat, "that the post would come to Greendale once again, by rail, the way it did when I was a boy."

"If they put the rest of the line back," said Sara, "perhaps the trains will come all the way up to Greendale once more."

"That can be a story for Julian to tell," said Pat, "when he's a man."

All the stories

"What can we do," said Julian, "when we have had all the stories in the story box?"

"We can put new things in it," said Pat.

"What can we put in?"

"You could begin with some bobbins," said Pat.

"And a bobbin-tractor," said Julian. "And the railway tickets, and the new ark."

"Yes, and then when *you* have a boy or girl of your own, you can tell them your stories."

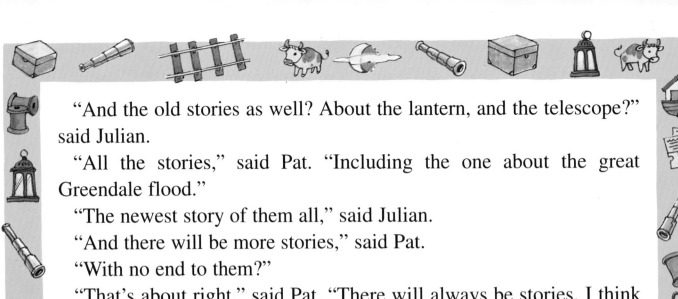

"And the old stories as well? About the lantern, and the telescope?" said Julian.

"All the stories," said Pat. "Including the one about the great Greendale flood."

"The newest story of them all," said Julian.

"And there will be more stories," said Pat.

"With no end to them?"

"That's about right," said Pat. "There will always be stories. I think we're going to need a bigger story box."

"That's all right, then," said Julian, snuggling down under the blankets.

"Goodnight, Dad!"

"Goodnight, Julian."

Julian was soon asleep, dreaming of stories and stories yet to come.